CRAZY TIMES
AT
CAMP CUSTER

JAMES MARSHALL

SCHOLASTIC INC.
New York Toronto London Auckland Sydney
Mexico City New Delhi Hong Kong

For Chip Hughes

Originally published under the title *The Cut-Ups at Camp Custer*
by James Marshall

ISBN 0-439-11199-4

12 11 10 9 8 7 6 5 4 3 2 1   9/9 0 1 2 3 4/0

Printed in the U.S.A.   23

Set in Aster

School was out for summer vacation.

Spud Jenkins and Joe Turner, a couple of cut-ups,

were first to leave the building.

It had been a rough year.

"Old Man Spurgle was really out to get us," said Joe.

"You can say that again!" said Spud.

Principal Lamar J. Spurgle took special delight
in curtailing the boys' activities.

Spud and Joe had spent more time in the principal's office than anyone in the history of education.

And to make matters worse, Spurgle made house calls.

But that was all in the past.

"Summer camp starts tomorrow!" said Joe.

The next day their moms drove them to Camp Custer. "That camp will never be the same," said Spud's mom.

"Jenkins and Turner," said a camp counselor,
"You're in Cabin Number Five."

"Hot dog!" said Joe.
"They didn't separate us."

The other campers in Cabin Five were a great bunch of guys.

"Look!" said Joe. "There's Mary Frances Hooley!"
"Who's that with her?" said Spud.

Mary Frances introduced Charles Andrew Frothingham.

"Charmed, I'm sure," said Frothingham.

"Charles is a fourth year camper," said Mary Frances.
"He knows all the ropes."

"I win Best Camper every year," said Frothingham.

"Big deal," said Spud.

"My uncle is camp director," said Frothingham.

"Big deal," said Joe.

"Here comes Uncle now," said Frothingham.

A helicopter circled the camp and landed.

The door opened, and out stepped...

"Oh, no!" cried Spud. "It *can't* be!"

"Well, well, well," said Lamar J. Spurgle.

"This *is* a surprise."

"You can say that again," said Spud.

"Uncle Lamar is the best camp director in the whole country," said Frothingham.

"Correct, Charles Andrew," said Spurgle.

"And I want *you* to help me keep these two cut-ups in line."

"Roger," said Frothingham.

"Of all the rotten luck," said Joe.

"Maybe it's just a dream," said Spud.

"We'll have to be extra careful," said Joe.

"We don't want to get sent home."

Late that night, when all the lights in Camp Custer
were out, someone thought it would be wild
to pour bubble bath in the wishing well and turn on
a hose – full blast.

The next morning Lamar J. Spurgle was fit to be tied.

"Gosh, Uncle Lamar," said Frothingham.

"Who could have done such an immature thing?"

"I don't have to think twice," said Spurgle.

Spud and Joe were put to work cleaning up the mess.

"But we're innocent," said Spud.

"No talking," said Frothingham.

"Or I'll tell Uncle Lamar."

The next morning Lamar J. Spurgle found some long
slimey plastic worms in his flap jacks.

"Gosh, Uncle Lamar," said Frothingham.

"Did those cut-ups have anything to do with this?"

Spud and Joe were assigned to baby-sit
Lamar J. Spurgle's repulsive dog Bessie.
"But we didn't *do* anything," said Joe.
"Come, my dear," said Frothingham to Mary Frances.

A few nights later, over in the girls' section,
something perfectly hideous peeked in a window and
cried, "Boo!"
The girls were upset.

"Know anything about this, boys?" said Spurgle.

"We're heavy sleepers," said Joe.

But Spurgle was not convinced.

And the boys were confined to their quarters.

"We're being framed," said Spud.

"And I think I know who's behind it."

"We'll just have to catch him in the act," said Joe.

Around midnight they heard some activity outside.

"Let's investigate," whispered Joe.
Slipping out of the cabin, they crept down to the lake
and hid in the bushes.
"Aha!" said Spud. "It's Mary Frances!"

"So *you* have been pulling those pranks!" said Joe.

"Don't be ridiculous," said Mary Frances.

"I have more important things on my mind."

"Where'd you get that neat boat?" said Spud.

"I made it in crafts class," said Mary Frances.

"Can we drive it?" said Joe.

"Maybe tomorrow," said Mary Frances.

"I have to make a few adjustments to the rockets."

And she carefully camouflaged the boat.

"Now don't get any funny ideas," she said.

"Oh we won't," said Spud and Joe.

But later that night they slipped back.

"The boat's gone!" cried Spud. "It *was* here!"
Suddenly Mary Frances was on the scene.
"What have you done with my boat?" she cried.

"We didn't touch your old boat," said Joe.
"I can make you talk!" said Mary Frances.
"Shh," said Spud. "I hear someone."

Charles Andrew Frothingham was just stepping into the laundry room with a big bag of itching powder.

"Aha!" cried Spud, Joe, and Mary Frances.

"So *you've* been pulling those pranks!"

"Can't we make a deal?" whined Frothingham.

"What's that noise?" said Spud.

Mary Frances's speedboat roared into view.

"Holy smoke!" said Spud.

"Who's that at the controls?" said Joe.

"Help!" cried a voice. "I can't stop this thing!"

The powerful boat tore around the lake.

It began to pick up speed.

"It's heading straight for us!" cried Joe.

"Duck, everybody!" cried Spud.

After the first week of camp, the boys called home.

"Is anything wrong?" said Joe's mom.

"Oh, there have been a few ups and downs," said Joe.

"But now we have everything under control."